No Room For Nicky

No Room For Nicky

by Alicia Kaufmann
pictures by Vicki de Larrea

Hawthorn Books, Inc.   Publishers   New York

For Marguerita

First Edition: 1969

When Nicky got into his crib,
he liked to have company.

First he had his blanket, his soft old blanket. It was a little bit torn and a little bit worn. It felt nice when it tickled his nose or rubbed against his face.

Nicky and Blanket went to bed
together.

Then Animal came along.
Animal was sort of fuzzy and
sort of floppy and looked like a
monkey. Nicky could put his
whole hand inside Animal and
make the paws clap together.
That made the head nod, too.
Then Nicky would touch the
smudgy old face with his nose
and say, "Hi, Sweetie-Pie!"

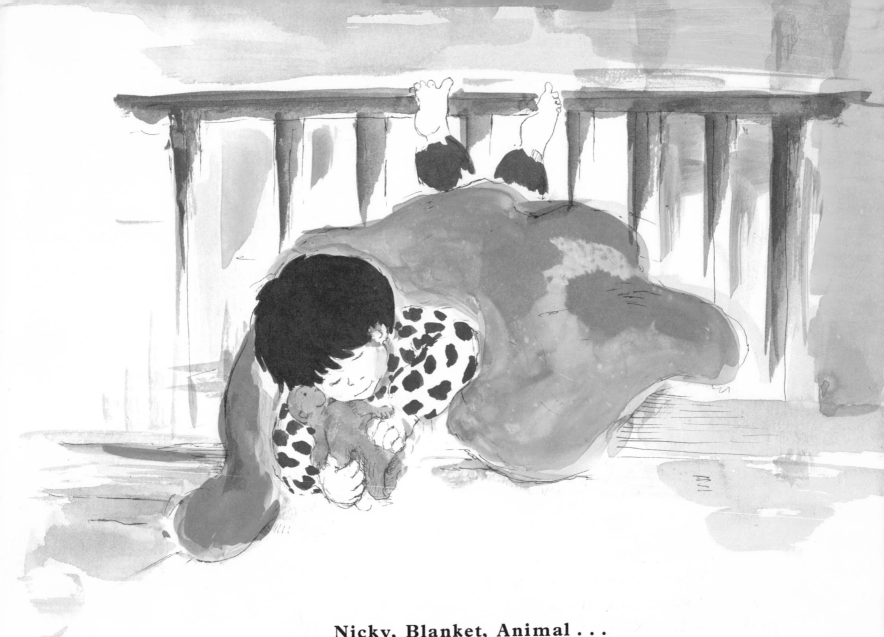

Nicky, Blanket, Animal . . .
they all slept together.

Next there was Kitty Cat. Kitty
Cat had red trousers and a
yellow shirt. Kitty Cat had thin
whiskers and a pink nose. Kitty
Cat was rough and tough and
didn't mind a strong squeeze.

Nicky, Blanket, Animal, Kitty
Cat . . . they all slept together.

Soon Nicky brought Russian
Doll in to join them. Russian
Doll was a plump lady made of
wood. She just fitted into the
roundness of Nicky's bent arm.
She was smooth and shiny and
painted all over with bright
colors and decorations. When
Nicky opened her up, there were
three more Russian ladies
nesting inside her.

Nicky, Blanket, Animal, Kitty
Cat, Russian Doll . . . they all
slept together.

Nicky had a small metal dump truck with black rubber wheels. He decided he really needed his truck with him, too. So in it came. But it didn't stay there long. In the dark and quiet of the night, Nicky bumped it with his elbow and it started rolling.

It rolled right between the
bars of the crib and tumbled
down onto the floor—CLINKETY
CLANK.

Nicky's father came in to see what had happened. He had his pajamas on and walked in a slow, sleepy way. He picked up the dump truck and put it back in the crib because that's what Nicky wanted.

Nicky, Blanket, Animal, Kitty
Cat, Russian Doll, Dump Truck
. . . they all slept together.

Nicky got a new box of crayons and a pad of paper. He liked to try all the colors and put the crayons away in their special box. He liked them so much he wanted to take them and the paper to bed with him. He spread everything out in a row in his crib.

When his mother kissed him goodnight, Nicky said, "Kiss Blanket and Animal and Kitty Cat and Russian Doll and Dump Truck and Crayons and Paper." So she did.

Then one night Big Teddy
came in, too. There they were,
all together: Big Teddy, Paper
and Crayons, Dump Truck,
Russian Doll, Kitty Cat, Animal,
and Blanket.

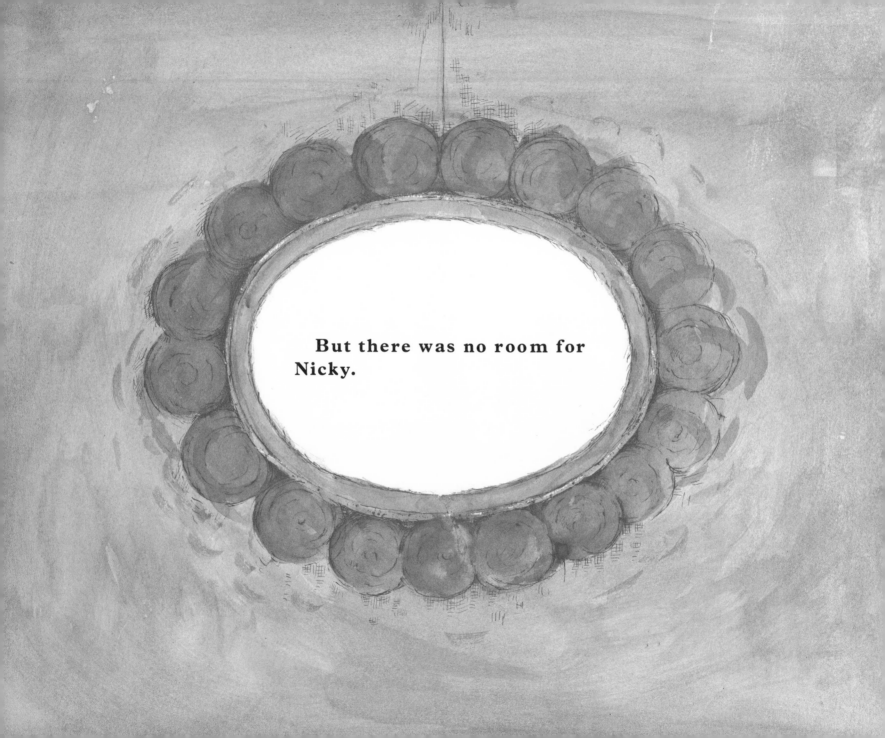

But there was no room for Nicky.

"I need a new bed!" he shouted.

"I think you do," said his mother. "This crib is getting so crowded. And you're getting so big. You need a new bed, just for you."

The new bed had its own soft
blanket and a puffy pillow and a
red bedspread. It had smooth
white sheets for Nicky to slide
in between. There was lots of
room now to turn and wiggle
and stretch and even do
somersaults.

And just so he wouldn't be too
lonely, right near his new bed on
a long shelf was a special place
for Blanket and Animal and
Russian Doll and Dump Truck
and Crayons and Paper and Big
Teddy, too. They were all
together.

But something was missing
from that shelf.

What was it? And where could
it be? Nicky knew. Do you?

ABOUT THE AUTHOR

Alicia Kaufmann was born in Philadelphia, Pennsylvania. She is a graduate of Queens College and is currently working toward an M.A. degree in Early Childhood at the Bank Street College of Education.

In addition to a life-long interest in writing, Mrs. Kaufmann has also worked in children's book publishing. Mrs. Kaufmann is married to John Kaufmann, an author, artist, and illustrator. They and their two sons live in Fresh Meadows, New York.

ABOUT THE ARTIST

Vicki de Larrea, a native New Yorker, studied at the Tyler School of Art in Philadelphia. She is currently attending Queens College.

Mrs. de Larrea has illustrated children's books for many of the major publishers. She and her husband, John J. Larrea, a photographer, live in Jamaica, New York, with their son.

PZ7
.K376N6

255250